WHAM-BAM-
Jelly-AND-Jam!
MY NAME IS CASPER, BUT MY BEST FRIEND, PETE, CALLS ME CARTOON KID.
DO YOU WANT TO KNOW WHY?
I'M AFRAID IT'S A SECRET, BUT – SHHHH – IT'S GOT SOMETHING TO DO WITH SUPERHEROES!* . . .
* KEEP THAT TO YOURSELF, OK?

JEREMY STRONG once worked in a bakery, putting the jam into three thousand doughnuts every night. Now he puts the jam in stories instead, which he finds much more exciting. At the age of three, he fell out of a first-floor bedroom window and landed on his head. His mother says that this damaged him for the rest of his life and refuses to take any responsibility. He loves writing stories because he says it is 'the only time you alone have complete control and can make anything happen'. His ambition is to make you laugh (or at least snuffle). Jeremy Strong lives near Bath with his wife, Gillie, four cats and a flying cow.

ARE YOU FEELING SILLY ENOUGH TO READ MORE?

THE BEAK SPEAKS
BEWARE! KILLER TOMATOES
CARTOON KID
CARTOON KID – SUPERCHARGED!
CARTOON KID STRIKES BACK!
CHICKEN SCHOOL
DINOSAUR POX
DOCTOR BONKERS! (A COSMIC PYJAMAS ADVENTURE)
GIANT JIM AND THE HURRICANE
THE HUNDRED-MILE-AN-HOUR DOG
THE HUNDRED-MILE-AN-HOUR DOG GOES FOR GOLD!
KRANKENSTEIN'S CRAZY HOUSE OF HORROR
(A COSMIC PYJAMAS ADVENTURE)
KRAZY COW SAVES THE WORLD – WELL, ALMOST
LOST! THE HUNDRED-MILE-AN-HOUR DOG
MY BROTHER'S FAMOUS BOTTOM
MY BROTHER'S HOT CROSS BOTTOM
THERE'S A PHARAOH IN OUR BATH!

JEREMY STRONG'S LAUGH-YOUR-SOCKS-OFF JOKE BOOK
JEREMY STRONG'S LAUGH-YOUR-SOCKS-OFF EVEN MORE JOKE BOOK
JEREMY STRONG'S LAUGH-YOUR-SOCKS-OFF CLASSROOM CHAOS JOKE BOOK

ILLUSTRATED BY

STEVE MAY

PUFFIN

PUFFIN BOOKS

Published by the Penguin Group
Penguin Books Ltd, 80 Strand, London WC2R 0RL, England
Penguin Group (USA) Inc., 375 Hudson Street, New York, New York 10014, USA
Penguin Group (Canada), 90 Eglinton Avenue East, Suite 700, Toronto, Ontario, Canada M4P 2Y3
(a division of Pearson Penguin Canada Inc.)
Penguin Ireland, 25 St Stephen's Green, Dublin 2, Ireland (a division of Penguin Books Ltd)
Penguin Group (Australia), 250 Camberwell Road, Camberwell, Victoria 3124, Australia
(a division of Pearson Australia Group Pty Ltd)
Penguin Books India Pvt Ltd, 11 Community Centre, Panchsheel Park, New Delhi – 110 017, India
Penguin Group (NZ), 67 Apollo Drive, Rosedale, Auckland 0632, New Zealand
(a division of Pearson New Zealand Ltd)
Penguin Books (South Africa) (Pty) Ltd, 24 Sturdee Avenue, Rosebank, Johannesburg 2196, South Africa

Penguin Books Ltd, Registered Offices: 80 Strand, London WC2R 0RL, England

puffinbooks.com

First published 2012
2

Set in Baskerville
Made and printed in Great Britain by Clays Ltd, St Ives plc

British Library Cataloguing in Publication Data
A CIP catalogue record for this book is available from the British Library

ISBN: 978–0–141–33994–8

www.greenpenguin.co.uk

Penguin Books is committed to a sustainable future for our business, our readers and our planet. This book is made from paper certified by the Forest Stewardship Council.

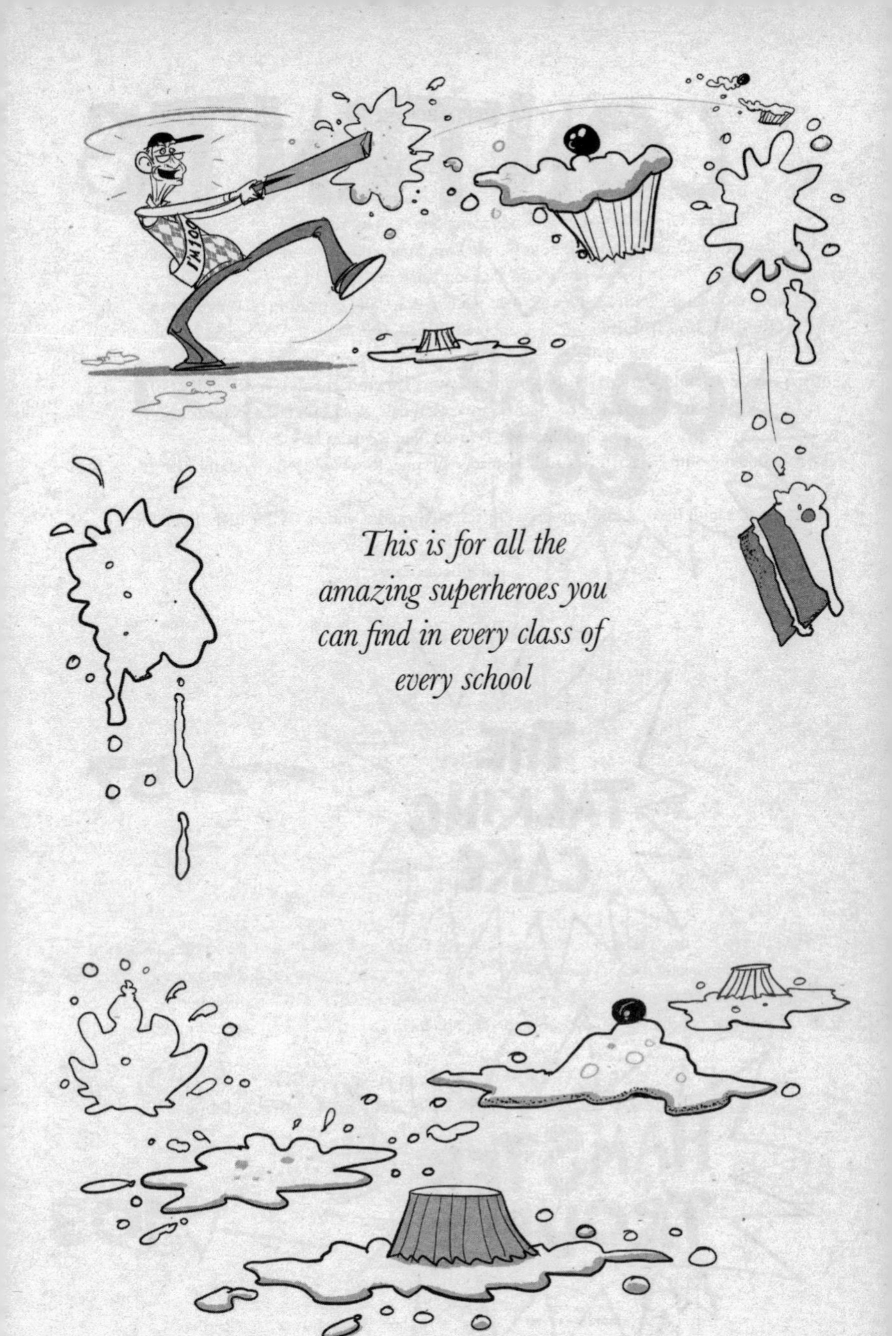

This is for all the amazing superheroes you can find in every class of every school

CONTENTS

GO, DAD, GO!

YESSSSs!

That's the noise our teacher makes when we do something brilliant, like a perfect cartwheel.

'He's doing his nut,' said Mia, who sits at our table.

'No,' grinned Big Feet Pete, 'he's doing his butternut!'

We fell about laughing because that's our teacher's name – Mr Butternut. (Except when he's cross with us and then we call him Horrible Hairy Face because of his beard.)

WELL DONE, CAMERON!

In case you are wondering who Big Feet Pete is, I will tell you. He is my best friend ever. He lives next door to me and he's got feet as big as surfboards AND, guess what? He's in love with Mia. Ha ha! I bet they get married. (And they're only nine!)

And now I will tell you why Mr Butternut was so excited. It was because our friend Cameron had just jumped from

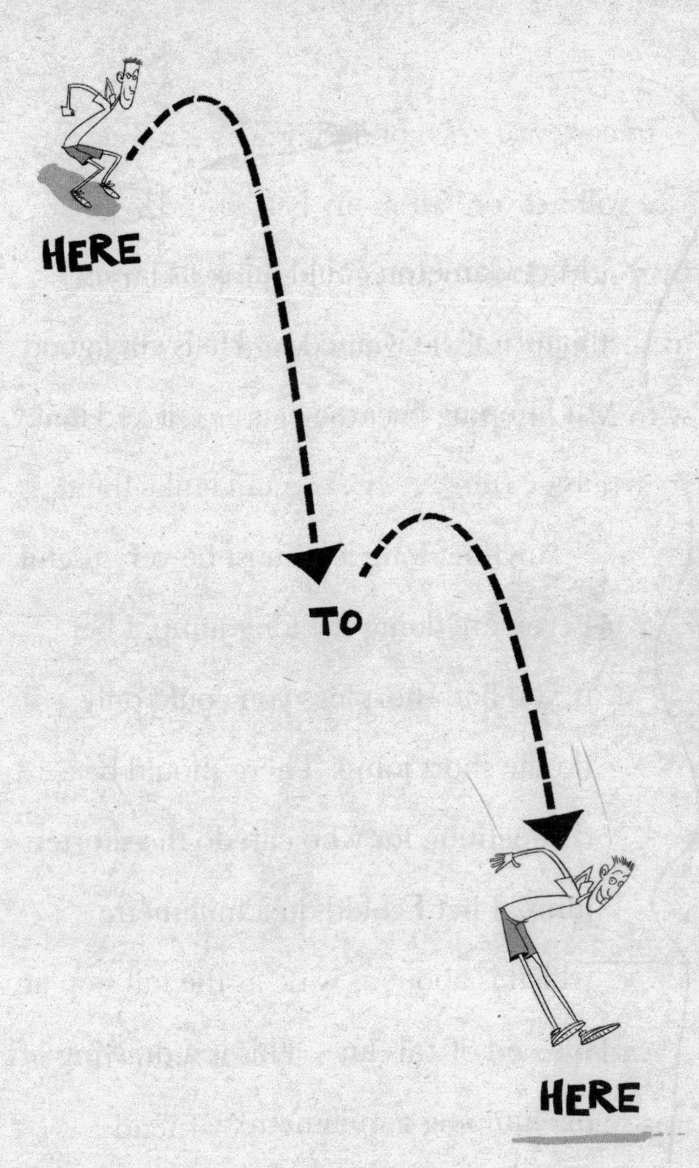

– which is a very long way indeed.

I bet Cameron could jump as far as Saturn if he wanted to. He is very good at jumping because he's as tall and lanky as . . . um . . . er . . . a tall lanky thing.

Anyhow, long legs must be very useful if you are doing the long jump. I bet if you had short legs you could only do the short jump. There should be a competition for who can do the shortest jump. I bet I could do a millimetre, which is about as wide as the full stop at the end of this line. This is a drawing of me jumping a millimetre.

See? I jumped such a short way you didn't even see me move, did you? I'm pretty good at drawing. The other kids in class call me Cartoon Kid because I draw all the time. (Even when I'm not supposed to – hee hee!) I like drawing my friends, especially my biggest best friend ever, Pete. He has a humongous nose, as well as those mega-sized feet! I've got lots of friends and they are ALL superheroes because that's what our teacher, Mr Butternut, told us when we joined his class. He jumped on to his desk and yelled –

WHAM-BAM-
Jelly-AND-Jam!
SUPERHEROES!
CAPES
BOOKS R COOL

TOGETHER WE WILL FIGHT INJUSTICE AND SAVE THE WORLD FROM RICE PUDDING AND OTHER HORRIBLE THINGS!!

That Mr Butternut is pretty cool, I think.

Anyhow, Pete and I invented superhero names for most of the class. That's why I'm Cartoon Kid and my friend Pete is Big Feet Pete. Mia is Curly-Wurly-Girly because she has THE MOST curly hair.

She looks as if a giant plate of spaghetti has fallen on her head. And Cameron – the tall boy with the long legs who had just jumped from

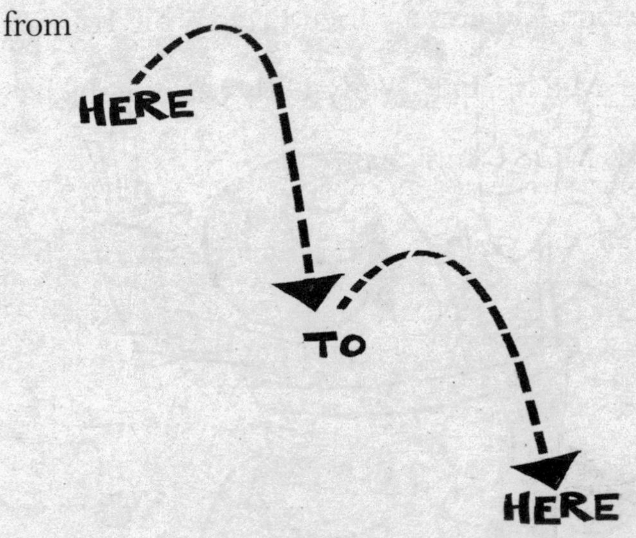

– is called Big Friendly Cameron or the BFC, because he's big and friendly, like the Big Friendly Giant, only he's Cameron. Obviously. Cameron is friendly to everything. He even hugs trees. And lamp posts. He hugged one of

the dinner ladies once. She was so astonished she screamed and almost fainted from the shock. She had to go home early to recover.

Mr Butternut was mightily pleased when Cameron jumped all that way. That is because we have Sports Day coming up and everyone is practising like crazy. There are people jumping all over the place and running everywhere. It's like the school has been taken over by hundreds of giant rabbits. Jump jumpity jump. Hop hippity hop. Run bunnity run.

I'm in the obstacle race. We do it in teams and I'm with Pete, Mia and Lucy. Lucy has ginormous braces on her teeth that make her lisp. We call her The Mighty Munch and she's amazing at gym. She can do backflips without getting dizzy. The last time I tried to do a backflip I crashed into Pete and gave him a nosebleed. He wasn't very pleased.

Anyhow, at breaktimes we've been practising doing obstacle races in the playground. You have to clamber up to the top of the climbing frame and down the other side, scrabble under the bench nearby,

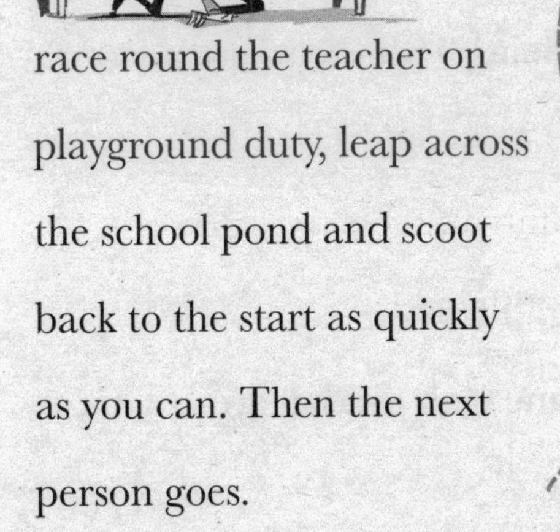

race round the teacher on playground duty, leap across the school pond and scoot back to the start as quickly as you can. Then the next person goes.

It's good fun – or at least it *was* good fun until Masher McNee caught sight of us. Masher's got a gang called the Monster Mob and he looks like a bulldozer on legs. He behaves like one too. He even makes bulldozery noises.

BRRRRR-GRRRRR-SKRRRKKK-URRRGGG-NEEYAAAH!

'What are you doing?' Masher demanded.

'Playing,' I said.

'Playing what?'

'Playing playing,' I said.

Masher drilled me with his dull eyes. 'That's stupid,' he told me.

'Yeah,' I nodded, because you *never* argue with Masher unless you want to be mashed into the messiest mash ever by him and his Monster Mob.

Bingo! He'd finally managed to work out the obvious. Then he began chuckling to himself. It wasn't a nice chuckle. It was a sort of hurr-hurr-hurrr laugh, a sneaky laugh, a THREATENING laugh.

'Hurr-hurr! Practising won't do you any good cos you're all a bunch of wimps. We're going to win everything.'

Mia stepped forward. 'You can't win the parents' and teachers' race because that's only for parents and teachers,' she pointed out.

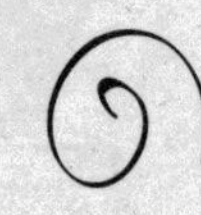

'That's what you think, spaghetti-head, hurr-hurr-hurrr. We've got plans.' And he went sloping off and the Monster Mob sloped off after him, with their shoulders all hunched up like vultures waiting to pounce on something. That Masher McNee is BAD NEWS.

We looked at each other. What did he mean? What sort of plans did he have? Then the bell went for the end of break. We went back to class and soon forgot all about it because Mr Butternut asked us if we had ever heard of someone called Jesse Owens.

Well, we all sat there looking completely dumb because of course we hadn't heard a peep – except for Sarah Sitterbout. She knows EVERYTHING. I don't understand how Sarah Sitterbout's brain fits inside her head. Maybe she spreads bits of her enormous brain round her body.

SARAH SITTERBOUT'S BIT ABOUT JESSE OWENS

Jesse Owens was an American athlete. He went to the 1936 Olympic Games in Germany. Germany's leader, Hitler, expected his athletes to win everything, but Jesse Owens won FOUR gold medals at running and the long jump and that made Hitler so cross he probably went cross-eyed and exploded because Hitler was a Mr Stupido and didn't like black people.

So Sarah shoved her hand in the air and told us all about Jesse Owens, and Mr Butternut grinned and said that was just how it was and that Jesse Owens was one of his heroes. And then Pete stuck up his hand and asked if that

meant Jesse Owens was a superhero like us, and Mr Butternut did that mad thing he does sometimes and he made ALL of us jump on to our desks and shout out –

After school Pete and I went home together. We have to go home together because we live next door to each other. Also, it's because Pete spends more time in our house than his own. That's because he's trying to avoid Uncle Boring.

Uncle Boring is not Pete's uncle at all – he's Pete's mum's boyfriend. His name is Derek and I have to tell you he is the most boring person in the WHOLE WIDE WORLD. He is always telling Pete what to do, or talking about buses he's been on, or hats he likes.

So Pete came to my house and we went upstairs to my room. I got my pet chameleon out of his tank and we all stared at each other. Chameleons are very good at staring because

Nothing wrong with my eyes. It's your eyes that are weird.

they've got bulgy eyes and they can look in TWO different directions at the same time. How weird is that? VERY weird, that's what. My chameleon is called Colin and he eats flies and other insects.

I said to Pete, 'Do you think chameleons ever think: *I wish I knew how to make some nice gravy to go with this fly.*'

'No, Casper,' Pete answered. 'I don't ever think that. But I do often think you are a knobbly-kneed twig-creature from another planet called Bumble-Wumble.'

'Thank you,' I said, because Pete's my best friend and I don't mind what he calls me because I just tell him he's got feet like a penguin. Then he tries to kill

me and I kill him back, so we're even. Anyhow, his nose is as big as a podgy potato AND he's got eyes that go all bulgy when he's excited and look like they'll go *SPING!* right out of his face.

Pete's got a pet too – Betty the hamster. She's always escaping and running off and eating the cushions.

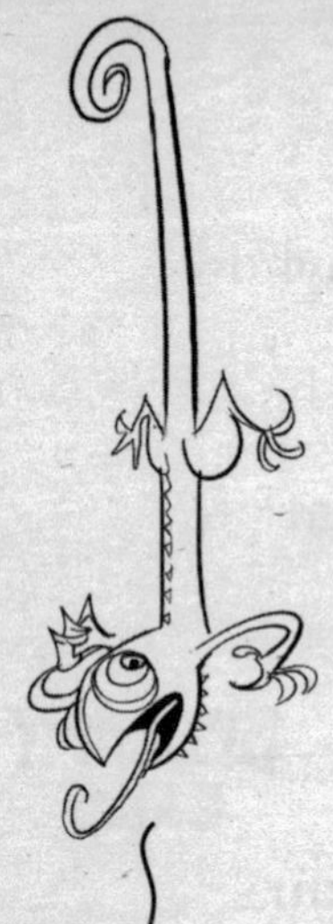

'I think we should practise for the obstacle race,' I said. 'We could start downstairs, race round the dining table, run across the sofa and leap off, up the stairs two at a time, dash into Abbie's room, jump on her bed –'

'Why do we have to go into your big sister's room?' Pete interrupted.

'To annoy her. Obviously. So we jump on her bed and hopefully she'll be in it, and then zoom back to my room and jump on my bed.'

Pete grinned. 'OK. Let's do it.'

We practically tumbled downstairs and went to the front room.

'I'll shout GO!' I said. 'Whoever gets back to my bed first is the winner. OK? GO!'

The first thing Pete did was try to push me over, the flaming cheat! I whizzed after him.

We bundled round the table,

bounced across the sofa,

thundered up the stairs,

and burst into Abbie's bedroom.

Abbie looked like she wanted to murder us on the spot so we dashed out – straight into MY DAD. Ooops!

'I've never heard such a row! Are you trying to destroy the entire house?'

I was going to say: '*No – just Abbie's room*,' but I am NOT Mr Stupido and I kept quiet and tried to look innocent of all crimes.

'Sorry, Mr Jenkinson,' muttered Pete.

'Whose idea was this?' bellowed Dad in his army sergeant voice.

Pete jumped in. 'Mine.'

Well, it certainly wasn't, was it? I was going to own up, but an amazing thing happened. Dad shut his mouth for a moment and calmed right down. He took a deep breath and told Pete that it wasn't a good way to behave in someone else's house and Pete wouldn't do it again, would he? Pete shook his head. Dad glared at me, turned on his heel and went back downstairs.

I let out a sigh of relief and turned to Pete. 'Why did you say it was your idea?'

Pete put a hand on my shoulder. 'Don't you understand anything? If you said it was your idea he would have killed you, right? He's not going to kill me, though, is he, because I don't live here. I guess I ought to go home anyway. Mum's probably made supper. With a bit of luck I might be able to frighten Uncle Boring away by putting a dead hippo on his plate.'

'Have you got a dead hippo?'

'Yes, I have, my tiny twiglet pal. I've tucked it under my bed. But I'll tell you something, do you know what Uncle Boring is planning to do? He wants to take part in the parents' and teachers' race on Sports Day.'

AAARRRGH! NOOOooo!

HOW EMBARRASSING IS THAT??!!

'But he can't do that,' I gasped. 'He's not a parent or a teacher! He's just your – I don't know, your boring uncle, I suppose.'

'He wants to take part,' repeated Pete. 'And I shall be even more embarrassed than I was when my trunks came off in the swimming pool last year. We've got to stop him.'

* * *

Sports Day arrived sooner than I thought and the whole school was on edge. Even the clouds in the sky looked excited. Horrible Hairy Face spent most of the morning telling us to calm down.

'It's like trying to teach a room full of monkeys,' he complained.

Mia put up her hand. 'Will you be in the parents' and teachers' race, Mr Butternut?'

'I certainly shall, and I intend to win it.'

'That's what my dad said,' Tyler announced.

'And mine,' added Cameron.

'Mine too,' I said hopefully, though Dad hadn't said any such thing, but I *wanted* him to.

'My father isn't,' blurted Hartley Tartly-Green. 'My father says running is a waste of time.'

'Not if Masher McNee is after you!' Pete blurted and everyone fell about laughing.

Everyone except Hartley, who always wanders round with his nose in the air as if the rest of us have been made from fart gas.

Lunchtime came at last and we had a final chance to practise our obstacle race. Masher McNee came wandering past, looking very smug.

'Just thought I'd let you know, my mum's in the parents' and teachers' race. So, I guess the result is pretty much in the bag. My mum's bound to win. Nothing could beat my mum.'

Pete must have felt mighty brave because he suddenly piped up. 'Want to bet on that?'

Masher's eyes narrowed to dangerous, knife-sharp slits. 'Yeah, bet you.'

We all looked at Pete. He smiled calmly. 'OK. I bet you ANY space rocket could beat your mum.'

We burst out laughing and Masher bristled with rage. 'That's cheating!' he roared.

'No, it isn't,' Pete answered. 'You said *nothing* could beat your mum, but a space rocket could, easy-peasy.'

'Yeah – or a cheetah,' added Tyson, which was daring of him. He's usually a real scaredy pants and wouldn't say BOO to a cheese sandwich, let alone Masher McNee.

'Or a Ferrari,' Cameron put in.

'Or my hamster,' Pete suggested.

'Of course my mum could beat your stupid hamster!' bellowed Masher.

'Not if Betty's driving the Ferrari,' Pete finished off.

'RRRRRRRRRGGGGHHHHH!' roared Masher. 'You're all stupid! You knew what I meant. Think you're clever, don't you?'

'Hang on,' I butted in. 'We can't be stupid AND clever.'

It was like watching a volcano struggling to erupt. 'You wait until this afternoon,' yelled

Masher. 'Then we'll see who's laughing!' He went storming off to find his Monster Mob. Maybe they'd help him feel better. Maybe they could have a group hug.

The trouble was, we'd had a good laugh at Masher for once, but we knew that would only make him even MORE determined to spoil things in the afternoon.

After lunch the mums and dads began pouring on to the school field and lining the racetrack. All the classes went out and sat on the field with their teachers, waiting to be called for their events.

The parents cheered and so did we, especially when Cameron won the long jump with his biggest leap ever. He went from

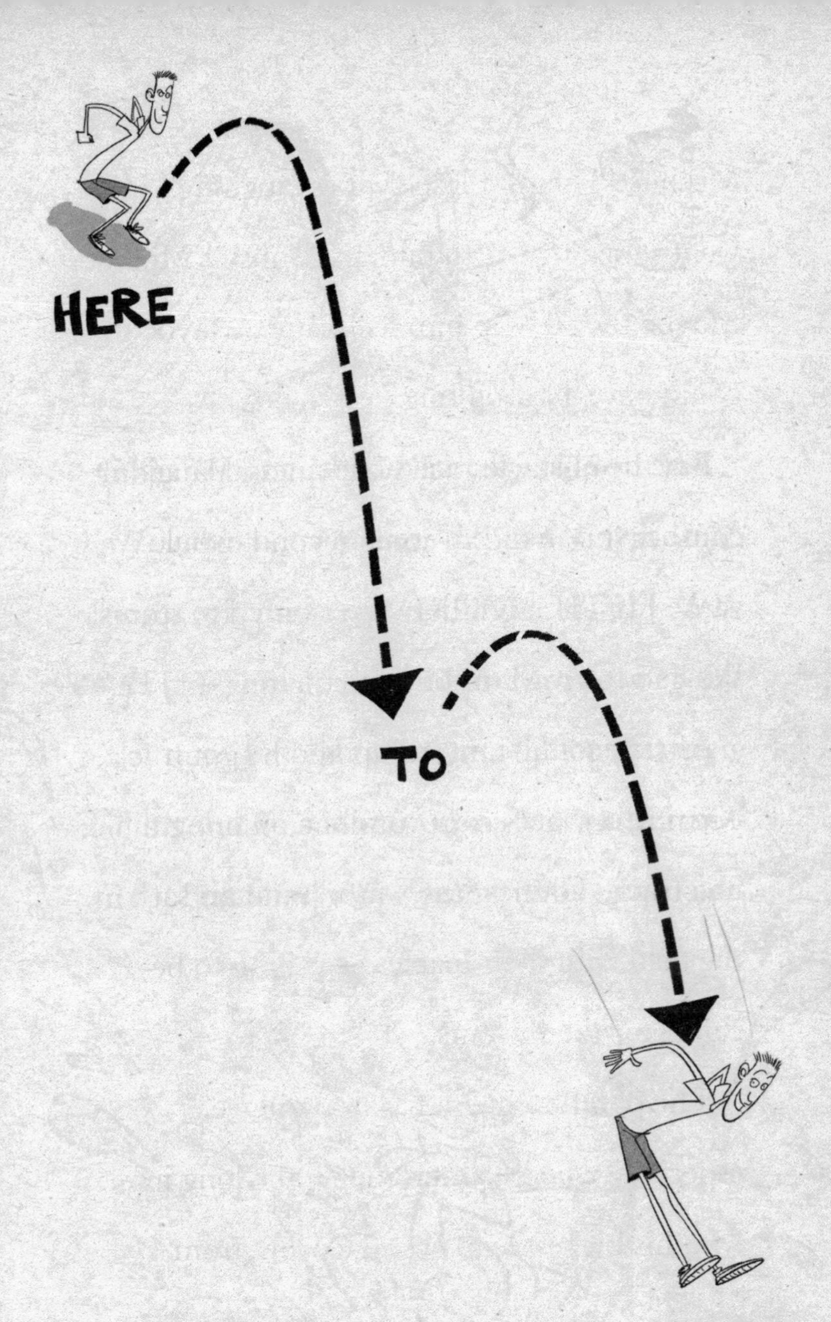
HERE
TO
HERE

But the obstacle race was a mess. We didn't come first. We didn't come second either. We came FIFTH, and there were only five teams! We had to crawl under some netting and Pete's giant feet got all tangled up and he got stuck. Then Mia's laces came undone on one trainer. She tripped over at the water jump and fell in.

Masher McNee stood at the side and laughed his head off. I wish his head really had come off. That would have served him right.

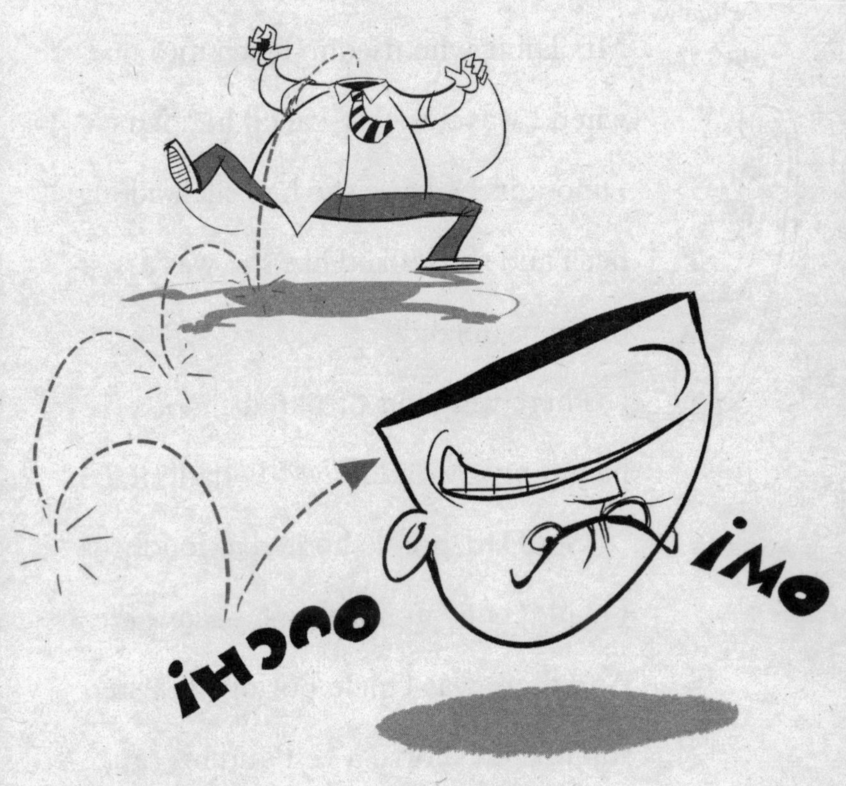

Then it was time for the parents' and teachers' race. Mr Butternut was there, jumping up and down and doing exercises on the spot. Miss Scratchitt, the head teacher, was there, and Mrs Dine, who used to teach me when I was five. (We called her 'Mrs Dinosaur' because she had such a long neck and she looked like she was a billion years old.)

Actually, she's 42.

There were lots of parents too, including my dad! Yay! My dad!

'Go, Dad, go!' I shouted as loudly as I could, but I'm not sure he heard me. And there was Uncle Boring, wearing small, tight shorts, a vest and his cap, looking rather silly. Pete hid his face in despair.

I noticed Hartley Tartly-Green looking to see if *his* dad was there, but of course he wasn't. For a second or two I felt quite sorry for him. And then I saw Mrs Masher McNee. Jeepers creepers, what a horrible heapers!

Mrs McNee had brought Jaws, the family dog. He has teeth the size of axe blades and bulging muscles and he looks remarkably like Mrs McNee herself, apart from the teeth. She handed Jaws over to Masher, scowled at everyone and got ready to run.

'On your marks, get set, GO!' yelled the starter, and they were off, hurtling up the field. Mrs McNee didn't run – she clumped, she thundered, she stomped and bomped and blundered. She elbowed people out of the way as she surged forward.

Uncle Boring had a strange way of running. He held out his hands like pistons on a steam engine. I wouldn't have been surprised to see steam coming out of his ears and a whistle – WHOOOoooo WHEEEEE! That Uncle Boring is VERY STRANGE.

But up at the front there was Mr Butternut and – guess what? MY DAD! Go on, Dad!

And who's that near the finishing line? It's Masher McNee! He's got Jaws with him. He's let Jaws off the lead! Jaws is racing towards the runners.

Jaws is going to eat them all! Oh no! There's only one thing to do. It's time for –

RUN FOR YOUR LIVES!
AAAAAAAH!

WE MUST DO SOMETHING!
I KNOW – LET'S RUN AWAY!

JAWS IS GOING AFTER MR BUTTERNUT AND YOUR DAD!

NO1 MUM
WE'RE COMING TO GET YOU!

BUT WHO'S THIS? IT'S CURLY-WURLY-GIRLY!
GERROFF ME, YOU HORRIBLE OCTOPUS!

SNARL!
GRRRRR!
CRUNCH!

OH NO! NOW JAWS IS AFTER EVERYONE!
GRRRRR!
I'VE GOT TO DO SOMETHING!
KENNEL
THIS WILL TRAP HIM!
TOO LATE, CARTOON KID! NOBODY CAN STOP JAWS NOW!
HELP!
HURR-HURR!
DEE-DOO! DEE-DOO!
DEE-DOO!
HOORAY! IT'S THE POLICE ELEPHANTS!
AND A POLICE KANGAROO TOO.
POLICE
IT'S JAIL FOR YOU, MY LAD!
KEEP STILL OR I'LL JUMP ON YOU!

SPORTS DAY ISN'T SUPPOSED TO BE LIKE THIS!
HURR! HURR!
No.1 MUM

It wasn't like that, though, even if it should have been. In fact something more amazing happened. Mr Butternut and my dad were trapped up the tree. Mrs McNee and Masher were chasing after Jaws, but they weren't

trying to catch him, they were just frightening everyone. Children were screaming. Teachers were shouting. Parents were gathering up their little ones. It was chaos.

And then, who should step forward to the rescue? Uncle Boring.

UNCLE BORING?!

We certainly weren't expecting THAT! He stood there, as stiff as a wardrobe, right in

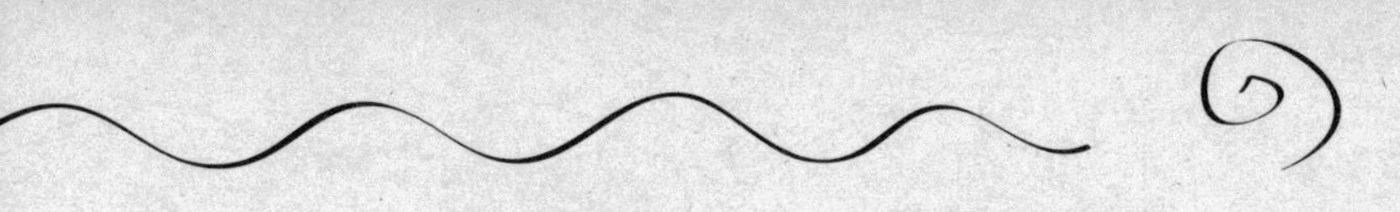

Jaws's path. The dog came howling towards him at hyper-speed, fangs at the ready and growling like he had a thousand furious killer sharks charging around inside him.

We gawped at Uncle Boring, astonished. So did Jaws. Uncle Boring quietly put a lead on the dog and handed it over to Mrs McNee. Incredible! That Uncle Boring was pretty brave. Or possibly not very bright.

'You'd better take that dog home,' Uncle Boring told her – and she did! Masher went with her too. Boy, did we let out a sigh of relief!

When Mr Butternut and my dad climbed down from their tree they were both declared winners of the parents' and teachers' race and everyone clapped them, especially me. My dad's got a trophy now. It's got a silver label on it that says: *Joint Winner of the parents' and teachers' race.* But between you and me I think it should say: *Jaws Very Nearly Ate My Dad's Bottom.*

As for Pete, he was strangely silent as we walked home together. Eventually he stopped dead and looked up. 'Uncle Boring just stood there. Why didn't Jaws eat him? I shall never understand adults. Or dogs.' He sighed deeply. 'Can I come to your house?' he added.

I grinned at my friend. 'Of course,' I said.

THE
TALKING
CAKE

NOOO!

Please, no! Please, no!

That was the noise I made when Pete and I were tidying my bedroom and I accidentally vacuumed up our class hamster. Am I Mr Stupido, or what?

WHERE DID IT GO?
IN THERE!
Sucker™
Catman
MARKER

It wasn't my fault – it was Dad's, and the hamster's. OK, so my room was a mess. My dad said that if we didn't tidy it at once he would call the Tidy Police and have us both arrested for Grievous Rubbish Making.

As for the hamster, I was supposed to be looking after it. Someone in our class always takes it home at the weekend and it was my turn. Why are hamsters always escaping? That's what I want to know! Pete's hamster, Betty, is always wandering off. He found her in the shower the other week. Anyhow, Pete said Betty was on the loose again too.

Our class hamster is brown and he's called Geronimo, which is a brilliant name for a hamster.

SARAH SITTERBOUT'S BIT ABOUT GERONIMO

Geronimo was a famous Native American Indian chief from the Apache tribe.

He fought the US and Mexican soldiers who were trying to capture him and managed to avoid them for twenty-eight years, so either he was very clever or the soldiers were pretty stupid. (Quite possibly both.) He escaped many times and was frequently wounded, but he always survived - at least he did until he fell off his horse in 1909, and died aged 80.

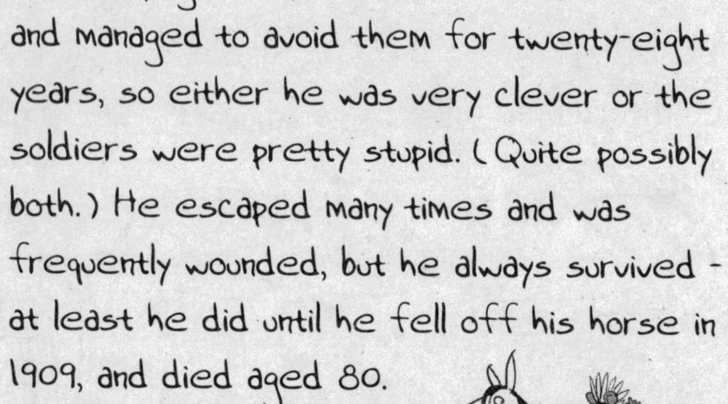

Geronimo is a very silly name for a hamster. 'Twinkletoes' is much nicer.

NO, IT ISN'T! IT'S STUPIDO!

I have no idea how Geronimo got out of his cage. Maybe some Apache friends helped him. Anyhow, it was MUCHO HORRIBLO. One moment he was skittering about the floor and then

SHWOOOFFF!

His little brown body suddenly went whizzing up the vacuum tube.

'Pete!' I yelled.

'What now, my knobbly-kneed twig-person?'

'I've just vacuumed Geronimo!'

Pete's eyes bulged. They puffed out so much I thought they would go **SPING!!** right across the room, like bouncy tennis balls.)

'Oh no!' he cried. 'Major emergency! Crash stations! Send for a hamster ambulance!'

'Pete! No! A hamster ambulance will never get up our stairs. It's too small!'

Pete was dancing round and round, waving his arms and generally behaving like some mad creature from outer space.

'Quick,' I gasped. 'Empty out the machine. Maybe he's still alive. Maybe we can save him.'

'Yeah!' Pete shouted excitedly. 'Then you can give him the kiss of life!'

I stopped and stared at my best friend. 'No, Pete. YOU can give him the kiss of life.'

'OH NO, CASPER! YOU can give him the kiss of life.'

'No,' I insisted. 'You can, cos your mouth is bigger than mine.'

'Yes, but your mouth is smaller and hamsters have VERY SMALL MOUTHS, so you would do it much better than me. Look, my mouth is way

This is definitely NOT a good idea!

too humongous for such a poor little furry thing. I would probably blow too hard and then he would burst!'

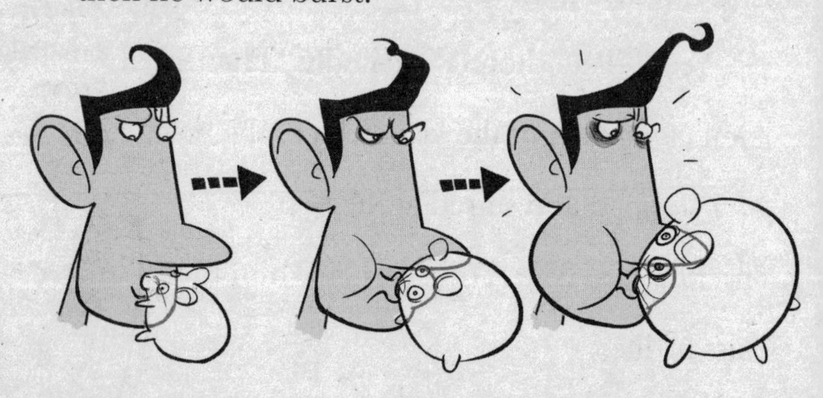

We glared at each other for a couple of seconds.

'JUST OPEN THE VACUUM CLEANER AND GET HIM OUT!' I bellowed.

We pulled every bit of that machine apart and yanked out the dust bag.

It ripped apart in our hands and the MOST REVOLTING, CHOKING DUST billowed out into the room.

We staggered around, choking and covering our eyes, while great clouds of murk and muck drifted round the room, slowly settling on everything – the bed, the chairs, the cupboards, the clothes and most of all, us.

'Not good, not good,' croaked Pete. 'Can you see Geronimo?'

I could, and I didn't like what I could see. There was a little brown thing poking out from beneath a pile of dust and cobwebs.

NOOOooo!

I bent down and very carefully pulled it out.

'Is that Geronimo, Little Twiglet?' Pete asked, and I nodded. 'Well, he looks a lot longer than usual, and much thinner. You should feed him more often. And by the way, Casper, have I ever told you that you are the Craziest Stick Insect in the solar system?'

'Yes, you have,' I answered calmly. 'And you are Mr Crummy Conk-Nose and your feet are the size of Africa.'

We were just about to start killing each other when we heard a tiny noise.

ACHOOOO!

I looked at Pete. He looked at me. We both turned and stared into the corner of my room. There, sitting on my bookshelf and rubbing his wrinkly-pinkly nose, was Geronimo. Hooray! He was OK. I'd never been so happy to hear a sneeze. The little hamster sneezed again. It was hardly surprising. He'd had half a ton of vacuum rubbish dumped on top of him.

I was about to make a grab for him when Dad put his head round the door to see how the tidying was going, and of course it wasn't. In fact the room was worse. A lot worse. And so was my dad. We got into deep doo-doo and by the time Dad had finished, Pete had been sent home and Geronimo had vanished yet again. That school hamster was a pain in the pants. Oh well, at least I knew he wasn't in the vacuum cleaner.

In any case, no sooner had I got Dad off my back than Mum was on it. She had a job for me.

Did you know my mum makes cakes? I don't mean for us to eat – she sells them. She is the best cake maker in the world and the house smells of cake in every room. (Except, of course, big sis Abbie's bedroom, which stinks of her favourite perfume. I think it's called MANURE.)

Mum had made a huge pile of fairy cakes. I have often wondered why they're called fairy cakes. Do you think it is:

A because they are made by fairies?

B because they have bits of fairy stuck in them?

C because they are small and light?

I think the answer is B – they've got bits of fairy stuck in them – lots of little arms and legs and bits of wing sticking out.

OF COURSE IT ISN'T B! I'M JUST JOKING!

So there I was, all alone in the kitchen with a huge pile of fairy cakes. Now then, what would you do? Would you:

A pinch a cake? (After all, they're only small.)

B pinch TWO cakes? (They're very small.)

C pinch THREE CAKES (because you're a big fat pig, you oversized fairy-cake thief)?

Anyway, that's quite enough with all these quizzes. What happened next was this. I had pinched a cake (only one) and was munching on it, when I heard

someone coming. It was probably Mum!

My mouth was still full of cake! Big Problemo!

I slipped under the table and squeezed right to the back out of sight. I peeped out and saw the kitchen door open. A moment later, who should walk in? Abbie. I'd know her big fat legs anywhere. (Actually she's not fat at all, but if you've got a big sis you have to say things like that, don't you?)

So big sis came wandering in. She closed the kitchen door and tiptoed across to the table. She was so close now I could have chewed her knees off. (YUCK! What a horribly knobbly thought!)

And then she began talking to herself! Ha ha ha! I'VE GOT A BONKERS SISTER WHO TALKS TO HERSELF! I thought I'd die laughing.

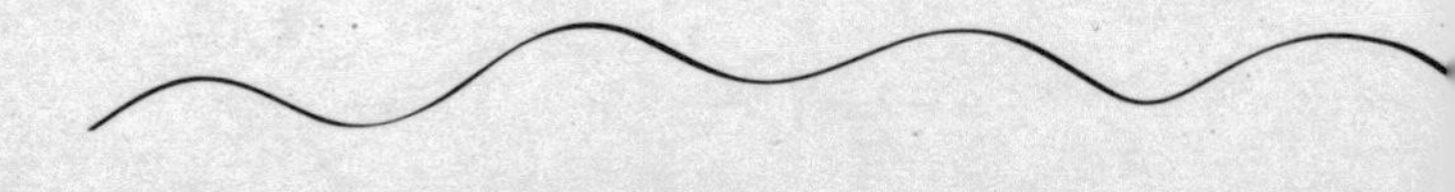

'Hmmmmm, Mummy's yummy cakes. They look utterly deeeeelicious. Now then, which one shall I have?'

She was just about to reach out for one when I gave a little squeak from beneath the table. 'Please don't eat me!'

Abbie screamed.

Mum walked in. 'What on earth was all that noise?' she demanded.

Abbie's knees were knocking together. I was holding myself as hard as I could to stop myself bursting with laughter.

'The cake spoke to me,' she said in a hoarse whisper.

'Oh, Abbie!' smiled Mum. 'Of course it didn't.'

'It did. It told me not to eat it. It even said "*please*"! Ohhhhh!'

'Casper,' said Mum. 'Would you like to come out from beneath the table?'

Uh-oh! I hurriedly wiped the crumbs from my mouth and showed myself. Mum folded her arms and fixed me with an accusing gaze.

'I understand you can do rather good talking-cake impressions,' she suggested.

Was that a tiny smile I saw her trying to hide? I think it was.

'Please don't eat me!' I squeaked again and doubled up with laughter.

Abbie snarled at me. 'Oh, ha very ha ha, I don't think. I knew it was you all the time.'

'OK, you two. We'll have no more of this,' Mum butted in. 'I'm in a hurry and I've a job for both of you. Gee-Gee's care home is having a special party this afternoon. The oldest chap there, Leonard, is celebrating his hundredth birthday and I have to get all these

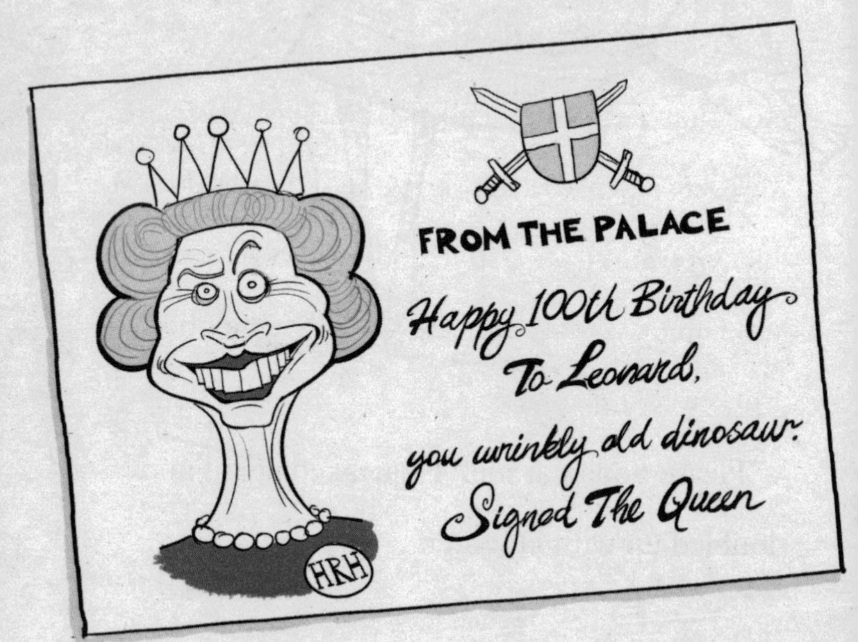

cakes up to the home. But I have to stay here baking. The pair of you can deliver these cakes. You can say hello to Gee-Gee while you're at it. Neither of you has been to see her for a while.'

I should tell you that Gee-Gee is my great-grandmother, which has got two Gs and that's why she's called Gee-Gee. Also she likes horses. (I bet she wouldn't fall off like Geronimo the Apache did.) Gee-Gee is amazing, even though she's into her nineties. She's a real live wire.

Abbie was already moaning. 'Do we have to go to the old people's home? It's full of old people.'

'That's what old people's homes are for, potato brain.'

Abbie ignored me. 'Do I have to do this with my idiot brother? Can't Shashi help me?'

Mum shook her head. 'No, she can't. The whole point of this is to get rid of you both. You've been moping about complaining of being bored, while Casper has been filling his bedroom with the insides of a vacuum cleaner.'

'But, Mum, the school hamster is lost in my bedroom and I've GOT to find him!'

'Tough. You can hunt for Geronimo when you get back. Take the cakes and go. And don't you dare eat a single one on the way! I have counted them and they'll be counted again when you get there.'

Huh. There was no escape. That mum of mine can be a real pain. The cakes were packed into a couple of cardboard boxes and off we went. Would I ever, ever, EVER manage to find Geronimo?

* * *

On the way to the care home we met Pete. As soon as he heard we were going to a party he wanted to come too.

'But it's for VERY OLD people,' I explained.

'I know, but your great-gran is amazing,' he said.

Abbie stared at him. 'She is a dinosaur,' she told him.

Pete grinned back at her. 'I know. I love dinosaurs. Aren't they stupendo?'

Abbie was speechless. She turned on her heel and went flouncing ahead.

Gee-Gee the dinosaur was very pleased to see us and insisted on giving both of us a big kiss.

YURRCKK!!

That great-granny of mine must be the world's slurpiest kisser.

'Stop whining or I'll give you another,' she threatened. 'Now then, bring those cakes through here. The party has already started.'

We carried the boxes through to the lounge. Music was being pumped out from somewhere. It was that old-time stuff; you know what it's like – wibbly-wobbly voices

singing about bluebirds and never meeting again and all that crumbly rubbish.

Leonard – the birthday boy, all of one hundred years old – was sitting in a big armchair, surrounded by cards. I think he thought we were deaf, the way he shouted at us.

The old lady beside him leaned across and shouted back in a wavery-quavery voice.

'I can't hear you, Lem, Lemmy, Lemon –' She shook her head hard and finally got it out. 'LEONARD!'

Gee-Gee spotted an old lady who was sleeping in the corner. Her head was tipped back, mouth open, and she was snoring loudly.

'Would you mind passing me a fairy cake, Casper?' Gee-Gee asked politely.

I thought Gee-Gee was going to eat it, but, oh no, definitely not. She took careful aim and lobbed it into the air. Pete and I watched in horror as it sailed

across the room until – **SPLOP!** – it landed right in the old lady's wide-open gob.

That great-gran of mine is definitely a big-time trouble maker!

'How's zat!' roared Leonard, cheerily waving his bat and getting to his feet. 'Good bowling! Chuck one my way!'

So Gee-Gee took another cake and bowled it at Leonard. He took a mighty swipe and sent the fairy cake zinging across the room at high speed.

'It's a six! Let's have another,' shouted Leonard. 'I haven't batted this well since I was thirty.'

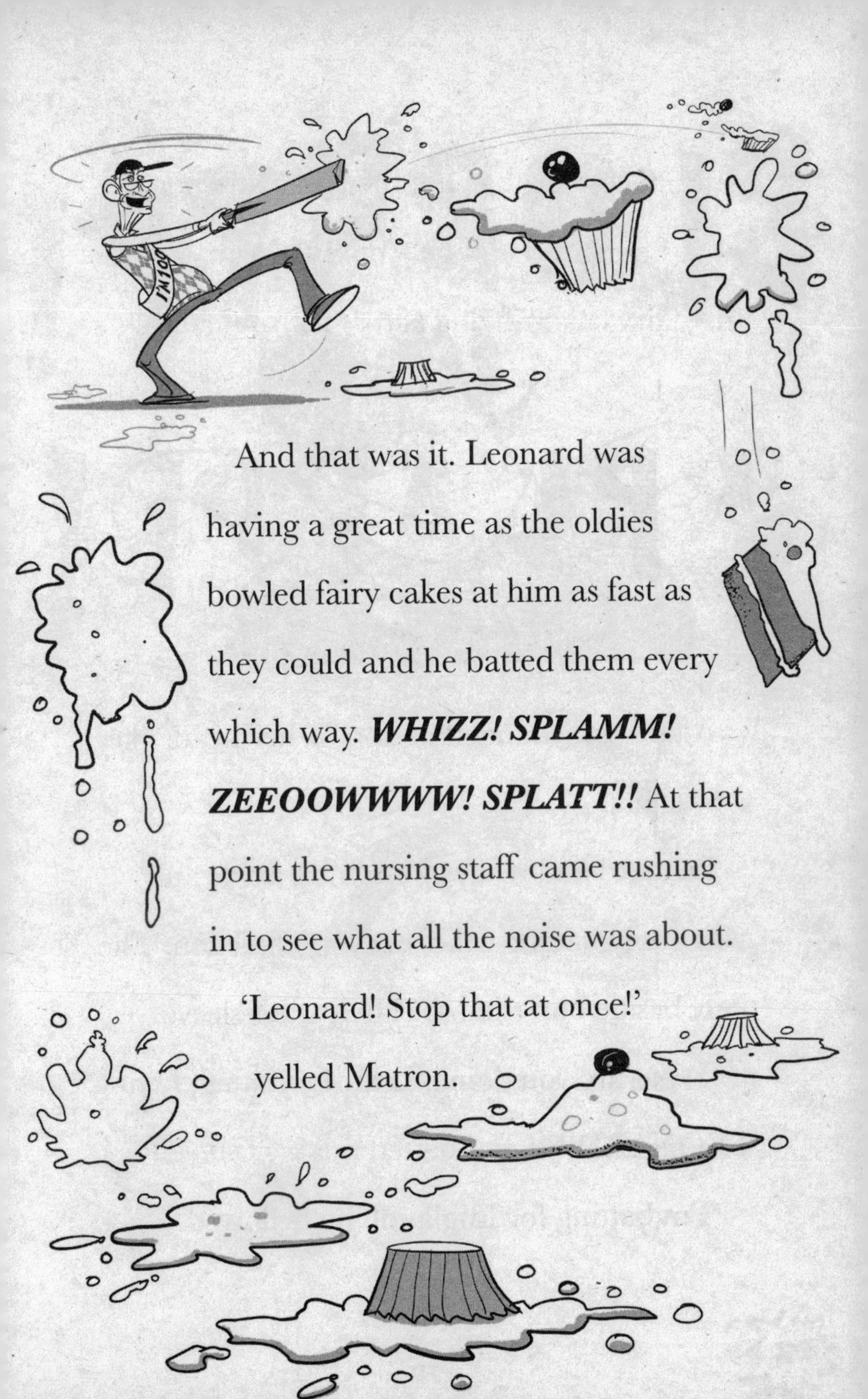

And that was it. Leonard was having a great time as the oldies bowled fairy cakes at him as fast as they could and he batted them every which way. ***WHIZZ! SPLAMM! ZEEOOWWWW! SPLATT!!*** At that point the nursing staff came rushing in to see what all the noise was about.

'Leonard! Stop that at once!' yelled Matron.

A fairy cake landed on top of her head, like a little hat.

Leonard had really got into his stride and was busily batting cakes in every direction. The lady beside him tried to clutch at his sleeve.

'What are you doing, Lem, Lemming, Lentil, LEONARD!'

'I'm batting for England!' he bellowed.

WHUMMPP!

Another cake hit its target and a nurse staggered back with cake, icing, crumbs and hundreds and thousands plastered across her chest.

'What do we do?' yelled Pete. 'We've got to stop them before they wreck the place!'

'There's only one thing TO do,' I shouted back. 'It's time for –

WE MUST GET THE BAT OFF THE WHIRLWIND WHACKER-BATTER!
I'M 10
EXPLODING CAKES! NOW WE'RE IN TROUBLE!
WHAT ON EARTH IS THAT?
IT'S THE TALKING CAKE!
ISN'T IT LOVELY WEATHER?
HELP!
DO SOMETHING, CARTOON KID!

TRY THESE!
HOWZAT!
BRILLIANT!

I CAN'T GET NEAR THE WHIRLWIND WHACKER-BATTER. WHAT CAN I DO?
BUT WHO IS THIS COMING TO THE RESCUE? IT'S SMELLY GIRL!
MANURE
MANURE

WHAT A PONG!
POOO!
MANURE
MANURE
THAT AWFUL STINK IS KILLING ME!

I'VE BEEN OVERWHELMED BY MANURE!

DO YOU LIKE MY NEW SHOES?
IGNORE IT.

ALL THE OLDIES ARE SAFELY BACK IN THEIR ROOMS.
PHEW!

If only things really had been like that, but, of course, they weren't. The nurses sent for reinforcements, which included three cleaning ladies, two cooks and the gardener.

It didn't take them long to wrestle the bat off Leonard and quieten everyone down.

Matron folded her arms across her chest and glared at everyone in the room as if we were all guilty of murder.

'Right,' she began. 'I want to know who started this.'

We all looked at each other and then the blame game began, starting with the old lady sitting next to Leonard.

'Len, Lennon, Lenin, LEONARD DID!' she blurted.

Birthday boy pointed straight at Gee-Gee.

'She bowled me a fairy cake!' he roared.

And Gee-Gee drew herself upright and stared straight at – guess who?

US!

'They did!' she declared. And all the other dinosaurs nodded their heads in agreement.

Now EVERYONE was staring at the three of us. Matron's eyes narrowed dangerously.

'Well, what have you got to say for yourselves?' she demanded.

'It's true that we brought the cakes here,' I admitted. 'But we didn't make them.'

'Then who did?' demanded Matron.

'Our mum,' said Abbie smugly. That big sis of mine was pretty smart to come up with that one!

Matron calmed down a bit when she heard that. 'I see. Right! Everyone get to work. I want this place scrubbed clean from top to bottom. Now!'

We were there for hours, at least that's what it seemed like.

When I was leaving, Leonard came over and patted me on my back.

'Blistering birthday! Best batting I've ever done. Must have scored a hundred runs, or rather – a hundred crumbs!' Leonard fell about laughing so much that it became a coughing fit. Then he almost DID fall over and two nurses had to help him off to bed. That Mr Leonard was a pretty cool dinosaur if you ask me.

So there we are. As soon as we got home I frantically set about searching for Geronimo. You'll never guess where I found him. He was curled up in the corner of Colin's tank, and so was Betty! How on earth did they get there?

HAMSTER TROUBLE

OWWWW!!

'ER?
WHAT?
OOOooH!
YURRRGHK!'

That's the noise my best friend Pete makes when he gets into bed and his feet plonk down into a warm, squidgy, rather furry

and the Mess bites him.

He yanked back the duvet. And what do you think he found? Betty, his pet hamster – and she wasn't alone. There were eight more hamsters with her.

EIGHT?!

Eight babies! I shall never babysit there!

What was she doing? Having a hamster sleepover?

No, certainly not, because the eight other hamsters were so small it could only mean one thing. Betty had just given birth to EIGHT BABIES! Octupletsters!

Pete came straight round to my house to tell me, still in his pyjamas.

NEITHER DID I, BUT THEN I DON'T UNDERSTAND HAMSTER LANGUAGE. MAYBE SHE TOLD ME BUT I NEVER KNEW. I PROBABLY THOUGHT SHE WAS JUST SAYING 'COULD YOU TIE MY SHOELACES?'
HAMSTERS DON'T WEAR SHOES.
THEY DO WHEN THEY PLAY FOOTBALL.
HAMSTERS DON'T PLAY FOOTBALL.
YES THEY DO, IT'S JUST THAT YOU NEVER SEEN THEM.
WHY NOT?

I looked at my best friend. 'Pete,' I said very seriously. 'Did you know that you are Mr Pudding-For-Brain?'

'No,' Pete answered. 'I didn't.' And he tried to clump me over the head with my pillow. So I grabbed his legs and we both fell over, crashed into the wardrobe and everything that had been piled on top – empty boxes, old toys,

spare cushions, football boots, a potty I'd had when I was two and half a dozen old games and puzzles that all had bits missing – came thundering down on top of us.

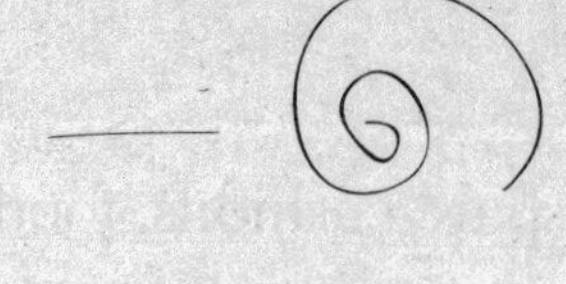

The next moment we had Mum, Dad and Abbie rushing into my bedroom to see what all the noise was about.

Dad glared at Pete and jerked his thumb over his shoulder. 'Home!' he ordered. 'And Casper –'

'– tidy my room?' I finished off for him as Pete slunk off downstairs.

Dad nodded. 'Exactly!' And he shut the door on me.

Huh! That's parents for you. It wasn't my fault everything fell off the wardrobe. What was all that stuff doing up there in the first place?

Wardrobes are for putting clothes IN, not for putting rubbish ON TOP OF. And who put it there in the first place? Me? Oh no. Mum and Dad. So it was all THEIR fault.

Typical. They cause the problem and I get the blame. Those parents of mine had a lot to answer for, if you ask me. Trouble is, nobody ever did.

I did some tidying. Well, it was more like shoving things under my bed where I hoped nobody would notice. I was still thinking about Betty and what I was thinking was – *Who's the father? Who could possibly be the dad?*

And then –

KER-CHING! DING-A-LING!

I knew who it was.

GERONIMO! Our class hamster. I couldn't wait to tell everyone at school!

* * *

Mr Butternut was very surprised to hear that Geronimo was the father of Betty's babies.

'When did they get married?' he asked and we all exploded.

I laughed so much I fell off my chair. That teacher of ours can be pretty daft, if you ask me. Mind you, I do fall off my chair quite a lot. In fact Mr Butternut once told me I should make sure that when I grow up I don't become a mountaineer.

'Because you are always falling off things, Casper.'

'That's because he's Number One Twit-Person,' Pete called out.

'I thought you two were best friends?' said Mr Butternut.

'Exactly,' I grinned. 'I'm Number One Twit-Person, and he's Number One Biggest-Feet-in-The-History-Of-The-World Person.'

'Ah,' nodded Mr Butternut. 'I guess that makes sense.'

See? My teacher was very clever to understand all that. When I say things like that to my parents they just roll their eyes as if I really am Number One

Twit-Person, which, of course, I am not. Definitely! YOU understand, don't you? Of course you do.

I should tell you that our teacher likes to sit in the old chair in the corner of our classroom. It's so old it's got stuffing coming out of it. I think Geronimo escaped one day, got hungry and started eating the chair.

Mr Butternut sat down and we all gathered at his feet wondering what he wanted to tell us. It's usually something exciting, so we were getting jumpy.

I'VE SOMETHING IMPORTANT TO TELL YOU.

'At the end of this week,' he began, 'our class is going to give an assembly to the whole school.'

That was Hartley Tartly-Green, who has a brain about the size of a raisin that's been nibbled by ear wigs.

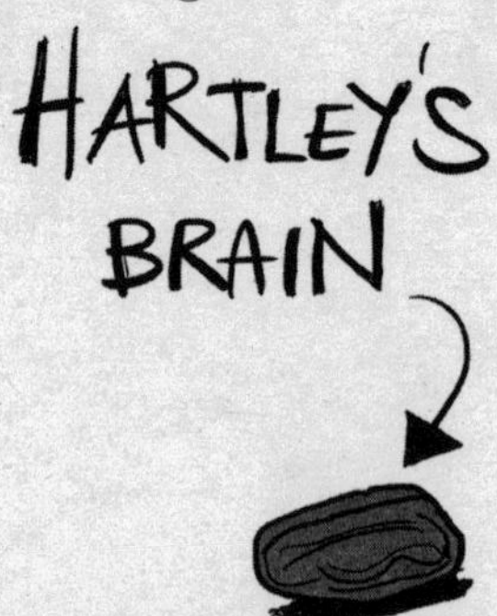

Mr Butternut continued: 'I have been wondering what we could do for assembly and I have come up with a great idea. Hamsters.'

WHAT????!!!

We looked at each other in despair. Hamsters? That would be about as exciting as watching snails go to sleep.

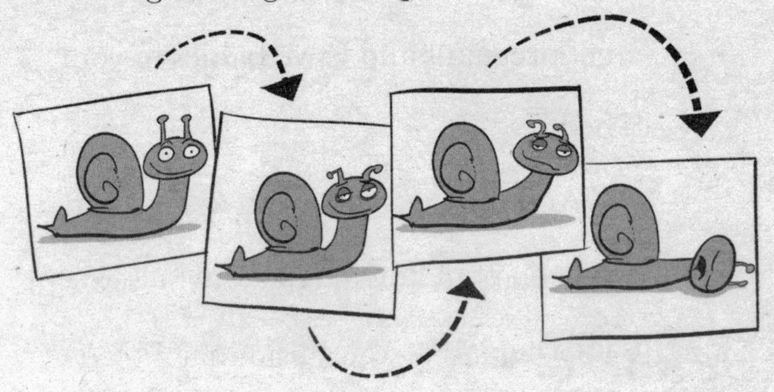

Liam was waving his arm in the air. 'Hamsters don't do anything,' he said. 'All they do is twiddle their wheels and do teeny-weeny poos that other people have to clear up.'

We all nodded in agreement. This was Mr Horrible Hairy Face's most boring idea ever, but he was still smiling at us and flashing his teeth.

'They do other things too,' he went on. 'For instance, we can talk about how to make sure your hamster doesn't get pregnant and leave babies in your bed.'

And then we all looked at Pete and rolled about laughing again – all except for Pete.

'It's not funny,' he said.

Well! Mr Butternut looked at him, showed two top teeth and slowly began to wiggle his nose like a hamster.

We just HOWLED! He looked so silly! We clutched our sides and this time even Pete fell over. He banged the floor with his fist! That teacher of ours is the BEST teacher EVER!

So that's how we ended up practising for our hamster assembly. Almost everyone in class had looked after Geronimo at one time or another, so basically we were a class full of experts. We all had something to say about hamster care. Our first effort seemed to go on and on AND ON until I thought that if anyone said the word 'hamster' one more time I'd scream.

I think Noella Niblet was as fed up as I was because she stuck up her hand and told Mr Butternut that if we went on like that during assembly the rest of the school would die of boredom. Noella's always complaining about something, but just for once I agreed with her, and so did Mr Horrible Hairy Face.

'You're right, Noella. We need action and drama. Why don't we turn all this information into a short play, a story – the story of Betty and Geronimo.'

'Stupendo!' we shouted and instantly set to. It didn't take us long to work out a cast list:

GERONIMO – *played by Pete. (We wanted Mr Butternut to do this because he wiggled his nose so well, but he said he was playing himself.)*

BETTY – *played by Mia. (Ha ha! Nice one! That's because Pete likes Mia and she's his girlfriend, even when he says 'No, she isn't at all.')*

THE BABY HAMSTERS – *played by me, Tyson, Cameron, Hartley Tartly-Green, Noella, Lucy, Liam and Madison.*

I wasn't too happy about Madison being a hamster because she's always sneezing and snorting. She does it so much that Pete and I call her Exploding Girl! But Mr Butternut said everyone should have a chance to take part. He smiled at Madison – she sneezed back at him.

Sarah Sitterbout did most of the writing. She is so clever. Sometimes I think her head must be about to burst. I bet there's so much stuff in her brain that bits of information are falling out of her ears like little wriggly things. Anyhow, Sarah can write faster than anyone else in class.

After that we had to think about hamster costumes. We cut out masks, painted them and tried them on.

'Bring some pyjamas from home,' said Mr Butternut. 'Try to make sure they are white, black or brown.'

'That's not much fun,' moaned Noella. 'Can't I wear my new pyjamas?'

'What colour are they?' asked Mr Butternut.

'Bright green and they've got big red strawberries all over them.'

Mr Butternut sighed. 'Noella, there's no such thing as a bright green hamster, let alone one that has pictures of strawberries all over it.'

'But they're my favourite, best ever ones,' Noella complained.

'Haven't you got some others?' asked Mr Butternut.

UH-OH! BIG MISTAKE!!

OH YES? A LIKELY STORY, I DON'T THINK!

That teacher of ours gave an even bigger sigh. 'Oh well . . .' he began, but he didn't bother to finish.

So on assembly day we brought our hamster pyjamas to school and we all showed off to each other. There were brown hamsters, and black ones and white ones. Tyson and Liam swapped tops and made themselves black AND white hamsters. And then there

was a bright green
hamster with bright red
strawberries.

We spent all of the first part of the morning rehearsing our play, especially the best bit, which came at the end, but I shall tell you about that later.

When we went out at breaktime, we were really excited and we kept our hamster pyjamas and masks on. Most of the other classes laughed and wished they were hamsters and doing assembly. But the older classes just sneered and made fun of us and said we were babies. I think they were jealous because when they did their assemblies they were just BORING BORING, LIKE MR McSNORING.

Meanwhile, we didn't realize that there were REALLY BIG PROBLEMOS going on, namely –

THE VAMPIRE TWINS – GORY AND TORY

They went flapping across the playground and surrounded Hartley Tartly-Green.

I know I get fed up with Hartley sometimes, but nobody deserves to suffer from the Vampire Twins.

'Hello, Hartley,' crooned Gory.

'We've got some chocolate biscuits,' Tory said.

'I bet you like chocolate biscuits, don't you? Yummy yum!'

Well, of course Hartley likes chocolate biscuits. EVERYONE likes chocolate biscuits. So the next thing is, Gory and Tory are slowly helping Hartley across the playground.

'Don't worry, little flower,' says Gory. 'Just pop in there and you'll find Stacey. She's got a WHOLE BAG of choccy biscuits and she's giving them away FREE!'

Now then, either Hartley Tartly-Green is an idiot, or he's plain greedy. (Or he's a greedy idiot!) He only goes and walks straight into THE GIRLS' TOILETS! Is he Mr Stupido, or what? And as soon as he gets in there the Vampire Twins push him into a cubicle and lock him in. Then they run off, laughing.

Noella Niblet goes in to see what all the fuss is about and then comes racing over to find us.

'Emergency! Hartley Tartly-Green is locked in the girls' loo! We've got to get him out! We've got assembly in ten minutes!'

Pete and I raced across the playground.

Cameron and Tyson came with us. We screeched to a halt outside the toilets. It was like Hamster Rescue Team are GO!

'We can't go there!' cried Pete.

'We've got to,' I insisted. 'We're doing assembly in a few minutes!'

We dashed in and hurled ourselves at the locked door. We banged it and kicked it and pulled at it. We even called it names, but it wouldn't budge.

'We'll have to get in there and help him,' I told the others.

'OK, but how do we do that with the door locked?' Pete demanded. 'Have you got a tank?'

'Just help me up,' I said. So Pete bent down and I stood on his back. I clambered over the top of the door, dropped down and – *SPLASSHH!* – my left foot went straight into the toilet bowl. Yuck!

I rattled the door furiously, but just like Hartley I couldn't find a way to unlock it. Then Pete got fed up with shouting instructions at me and he climbed over the door too. He was closely followed by Cameron, who managed to fall into the cubicle upside down. So now Scaredy-Pants Tyson was the only one on the outside, complaining that he couldn't climb over the door because he was frightened of heights.

That was when the Vampire Twins came swooping back. They crept up behind Tyson and –

BOO!

You should have seen him jump!

Now FIVE boys were jammed inside a cubicle in the girls' toilets AND we had the Vampire Twins waiting for us outside. There was only one thing for it. It was time for –

QUICK, CARTOON KID! DRAW SOMETHING!
I'M DOING MY BEST!
HANG ON TIGHT, EVERYONE!
BOOSTER
BOOSTER
5-4-3-2-1
LIFT OFF!
HA HA HA! WE'VE ESCAPED!
WATCH OUT, BOYS! THE VAMPIRE TWINS ARE AFTER YOU!
WE SHALL SOON HAVE YOU ALL WRAPPED UP!
HELP! WE'RE SLOWING DOWN!
I WANT MY MUMMY!

BUT WHO'S THIS? IT'S EXPLODING GIRL!
ACHOO!
HELP! WE'RE FALLING BACK TO EARTH!

SLOPP!
OH! I HAVE INTRUDERS IN MY ICING!
DEE-DOO!
DEE-DOO!
POLICE
WE ARREST YOU FOR WASTING TOILET ROLLS AND DAMAGING CAKE ICING.
WE ARE THE CHAMPIONS!

If only we really did have a rocket-powered toilet. What actually happened was that Mr Horrible Hairy Face turned up.

'Just WHAT is going on here?' he boomed.

'We're stuck,' I explained. 'The door's locked.'

'Just a moment. The caretaker is on her way.'

We heard the caretaker, Mrs Moppnot, arrive with her box of tools. She and Mr Butternut examined the door from the outside.

'It's simple, innit?' said Mrs Moppnot.

'Really?' asked Mr Butternut.

'Oooh yersss. Look at that there screw there.'

'Is it important?' asked Mr Butternut.

'Oooh yersss. Shouldn't not be there, should it? No. Not never.'

'Shouldn't it? Where should it be?'

'Shouldn't be not nowhere,' squawked Mrs Moppnot. 'Someone has put that screw in there and jammed the bolt on the other side so not nobody nor no one can open it. All I have to do is unscrew it like that and –'

BANG! The door flew open and out of the toilet tumbled five hamsters.

GREAT HEAVENS!

'What's all them giant hamsters doin' in my toilets?' cried Mrs Moppnot.

But there was no time to explain. We had an assembly to give to the whole school. Mr Butternut sent us scurrying back to class while he explained things to Mrs Moppnot. Then he came racing after us.

'I'll find out what really happened later,' promised Mr Horrible Hairy Face. 'Now get on to that stage and do your best.'

So we did. The play went really well, apart from my left foot making squelching noises all the time from having got stuck in the toilet. Everyone learned loads and loads about hamsters and how to look after them, especially about not leaving male hamsters in

the same cage as female hamsters, otherwise you will probably end up with far more hamsters than you could ever want. The other classes fell over laughing when we got to the best bit right at the end. (I said I'd tell you about this later, and now it's time.) Guess what? Pete and Mia GOT MARRIED!

It was a pretend marriage of course. All the little baby hamsters threw confetti over them. It was really funny. And Mia smiled at Pete and he went so red I thought he'd burst into flames. It was absolutely MARVELLISSIMO and the best assembly ever!

As for the Vampire Twins, they had to go and see the head teacher and were they in BIG TROUBLE? They most certainly were.

And that was the end of another brilliant day. The superheroes had triumphed AGAIN. I never know what's going to happen next when I'm in Mr Butternut's class!

It all started with a Scarecrow.

Puffin is seventy years old.

Sounds ancient, doesn't it? But Puffin has never been so lively. We're always on the lookout for the next big idea, which is how it began all those years ago.

Penguin Books was a big idea from the mind of a man called Allen Lane, who in 1935 invented the quality paperback and changed the world. **And from great Penguins, great Puffins grew, changing the face of children's books forever.**

The first four Puffin Picture Books were hatched in 1940 and the first Puffin story book featured a man with broomstick arms called Worzel Gummidge. In 1967 Kaye Webb, Puffin Editor, started the Puffin Club, promising to **'make children into readers'**. She kept that promise and over 200,000 children became devoted Puffineers through their quarterly instalments of *Puffin Post*, which is now back for a new generation.

Many years from now, we hope you'll look back and remember Puffin with a smile. **No matter what your age or what you're into, there's a Puffin for everyone.** The possibilities are endless, but one thing is for sure: whether it's a picture book or a paperback, a sticker book or a hardback, **if it's got that little Puffin on it – it's bound to be good.**